Jobe

Enjoy reading this
book as you grow up.

Anna Marie Squailia

This book is a tribute to the dreams I had as a child. The dreams I buried away because of hardships. But a different set of hardships caused me to find the courage to pursue those dreams. My hearts desire is for every child to know that no matter what hardships they endure they can still live their dreams.

I want to thank God for always being by my side through this journey. I want to thank my children Kayla and Isabella for being my inspiration to get this done. I love you both more than you will ever know. I want to thank my family Beverly Carney, Alan, Debbie and Richard Squailia. I couldn't have done this without your love and support. I also want to thank my ex-mother-in-law, who died last year. Every time we talked over the last 16 years she would encourage me to write a book. Thank you Nana Rose for believing in me and encouraging me. You are greatly missed.

The last person I want to thank is Michael Graham without you this book would not be complete. You are a fantastic artist. Thank you for all your hard work and awesome illustrations.

AnnaMarie Squailia

"I am amazed and impressed with the book as a learning tool. My own children go back again and again to the book as we work through the questions and activities. The adventures of the ugly duckling have resulted in great discussion in our family and I strongly recommend it!"
Michael Selby, Doctor of Education
Project Discovery High Performance Training

"The Hidden Swan lays the Seeds of Greatness in a Child's life."
Denis Waitley, Author, "The Seeds of Greatness"

"A perfect enrichment tool, blending the fun of reading with the opportunity for children to grow in understanding their own feelings and strengths."
Home Schooling Parent

"There is nothing greater you can do for your child than help them develop a love for reading. This book is perfect for that."
Charlie Tremendous Jones- President of Executive Books

"Through familiar classic folklore, The Hidden Swan brings an empowering message beyond the value of tolerance. The hidden strength of diversity is prompted and revealed in the topical questions and great discussion points provided with the story."
Mark Nason, Vice President, Alibris

"Our children are so valuable. Books like The Hidden Swan, is what this nation needs to raise great leaders."
Dawn Gibbons, First Lady of Nevada

"I strongly recommend The Hidden Swan to others. I am a mother of two boys and our entire family enjoyed this book. My oldest found it an easy read and enjoyed finding life lessons between the lines. My youngest loved the story line and coloring the pictures. I found the activities in this book extremely helpful parenting tips. I actually still am using some of these tips to this day."
M. Brantner, Mother of Two Boys

Copyright © 2008 by Successful Kids Publishing
Book adaptation by AnnaMarie Squailia
Illustrations by Michael Graham

Printed in the United States

Library of Congress Control Number 2007908062

Squailia, AnnaMarie
The Hidden Swan; A Tale of an Ugly Duckling's Journey to Learn his True Identity
and Ways You Can Too!!!/ AnnaMarie Squailia; Michael Graham illustrator
ISBN 987-09800431-4-3
Summary: An interactive book designed to enhance children's self-awareness while building relationship.
[1. Moral Education.   2. Values.   3. Children- Conduct of life.   4. Active learning.   5. Child rearing.]
l Title

Successful Kids Publishing
P.O. Box 34025
Reno, NV. 89533
www.successfulkidspublishing.com

Successful Kids Publishing

The Hidden Swan

A Tale of an Ugly Duckling's Journey to Learn his True Identity and Ways You Can Too!!!

Written by AnnaMarie Squailia
Illustrated by Michael Graham

It was springtime in the country. Dragonflies whirled, tadpoles wiggled, and eggs of every size and color hatched. In the tall grass along the riverbank, a tired mother duck sat on her nest. She stood and stretched, looking over her five beautiful tan eggs—and one large plain white egg.

She fluffed her tail feathers, settled back down with an impatient sigh, and said, "Hatching ducklings takes a long time."

Suddenly, she felt something wiggle beneath her. She bolted up.

Peck! Peck! Peck! The baby ducks began to chip away at their shells.

A hole appeared in one egg and a crack in another! The ducklings struggled to be free of their shells. They knew something better was waiting for them outside.

"Quack! Quack! Quack!" encouraged Mother Duck, dancing in excited circles. Crack! Crack! Crack! Three shells broke open and three yellow ducklings popped out, saying, "Peep! Peep! Peep!"

Crack! Crack! Two more ducklings emerged from their shells. One looked around with wide eyes and said, "My, the world is so big!"

"Wait until you see the pond and the farm," said Mother Duck. "Would you like to explore?"

"Yes!" peeped the eager ducklings, shaking off the rest of their shells as their yellow down began to dry.

Mother Duck gathered her brood, but stopped as she noticed that the sixth egg, the large, ugly white egg, hadn't yet hatched.

She plopped back down and said, "Oh my! We have to wait for your brother or sister to hatch."

Disappointed, the whole family snuggled in their nest and waited, and waited, and waited. The babies kept the egg warm while their mother went to find them some food.

It took one whole day before they finally heard the sounds of pecking.

Peck! Peck! Peck!

Mother Duck stood, danced in excited circles and said, "Quack! Quack! Quack!" Finally, the large egg cracked open and six pairs of eyes watched as the newest member of their family worked hard to chip away his shell.

Once he was free with wide eyes, he looked around and said, "The world is so big!"

"Just like you," replied one of the ducklings. "You're enormous!"

"And you look different," said another.

The last duckling shook off the rest off his shell and fluffed his down in the wind. He was big and a sooty gray compared to his tiny yellow brothers and sisters.

"You are different," said Mother Duck, "just like the egg you came from."

"I think he looks ugly," said one of the ducklings.

Soon Mother Duck led her babies to the pond. She jumped in. Splash!

"Quack! Quack!" she called and one after another, the ducklings followed.

At first, the water closed over their heads, but in an instant they bobbed back up to the surface and paddled with their little webbed feet. All of the ducklings loved the water, especially the Ugly Duckling, who swam so well that he was able to help his brothers and sisters.

"You must be a duck," said Mother Duck, "because you're a great swimmer and very helpful."

After they'd splash for a long time, Mother Duck said, "Let's go to the farm where they'll feed us some corn. Stay close and walk like me. Everyone stick out your tails and waddle!"

In the farmyard the Ugly Duckling saw a dog, a cat, some sheep, chickens, geese, and a cow. There were also other ducks that came to greet Mother Duck and her new family, but when they saw the Ugly Duckling, the other ducks honked and hissed at him.

One duck stretched his neck and flapped his wings wildly, shouting, "Shoo! We don't want you here!"

Then he bit the poor, frightened Ugly Duckling on the neck.

"Leave him alone!" scolded Mother Duck. "He's not hurting anyone."

"But he's so big and different," said the cruel duck.
"He doesn't belong here with the rest of us."

"He might not look like you or me, but he's a strong swimmer and very helpful," said Mother Duck. "I think he's going to be important when he grows up."

The Ugly Duckling hung his head low and thought, "Am I really that different?"

By the end of summer little had changed. Life was still difficult for the Ugly Duckling. While his sisters and brothers played with the other ducks, he was teased, bitten, and called all sorts of horrible names.

But the really terrible thing was that his brothers and sisters started picking on him. They said things like, "We wish you weren't here. If you were gone, all the other animals would be nicer to us."

The Ugly Duckling looked to Mother Duck for support, but she didn't know what to do. So she just turned away, pretending she didn't hear.

Heartbroken, the Ugly Duckling waddled to the edge of the farmyard.

"No one would miss me if I go away," he said to himself.

Then he ran as fast as he could, flapped his wings, and began to fly for the very first time.

When he thought he couldn't flap one more time, he saw a pond below. He flew down into some reeds.

Across the pond there were some wild geese swimming.

Then the Ugly Duckling had an idea.

"I know how I can fit in," he said, smearing
mud onto his feathers.

After a few minutes several of the geese swam toward the Ugly Duckling.

"What are you?" asked one goose.

"I'm just like you," the Ugly Duckling said hopefully.

The geese laughed and one of them said, "Just like us? Whatever you're trying to be, it's not working because you're definitely not like us!"

Suddenly, a strange thunder roared and echoed across the lake scaring the geese into the air. Bang! Bang! Blue smoke drifted across the water and hunters in tall rubber boots came trampling along the shore holding their guns.

Quickly washing off the mud, the Ugly Duckling hid in the tall reeds.

A moment later a big brown dog splashed into the water and glared right at him.

The Duckling shivered and hid his head under his wing. The dog just sniffed the Ugly Duckling but instead of biting him with his huge jaws, he turned and snatched a dead goose from the water.

The Ugly Duckling watched in terror as the hunters and the dog continued to make their way along the shoreline until they finally disappeared from view.

Although he was shaking with fear, the Ugly Duckling thought, "I'm so ugly that even that dog didn't want anything to do with me!"

Several hours later he thought it was safe to leave the pond, he ran in case the hunters were still nearby. Dark clouds began to gather overhead.

Soon, rain began to fall like pebbles on his head and back. In the distance he could see a rickety old cottage. He dashed through a door that hung from one hinge and into a dark stuffy room. He huddled in a corner and tried to sleep. But the pounding rain and rumbles of thunder reminded him of the roar of the guns at the pond.

In the morning the Ugly Duckling woke to the sound of a cat. "Hiss! Meow!"
And the cackle of a hen.

"Cluck! Cluck! Cluck! Can you lay eggs?" asked the hen.

"No," replied the Ugly Duckling.

"Can you purr and arch your back?" asked the cat.

"No," replied the Ugly Duckling.

"Then what good are you?" said the cat. "If you can't lay eggs or purr, the old woman won't let you stay here."

Just then, an old woman hobbled out of bed.

"What is all the fuss about?" she said, squinting through her thick glasses.

"My, my, what a large duck! You may stay with us if you lay eggs."

That night the Ugly Duckling was allowed to sleep in the cottage. When the woman, the cat, and the hen were all asleep, he tried to purr, but a horrible bellow came out instead.

He squeezed his stomach, trying to lay an egg, but nothing happened. He thought, "If I believe hard enough, I can do it," but try as he might, he couldn't lay an egg.

With tears in his eyes he looked out the window at the moon and thought, "Why am I so different? I can't seem to fit in no matter how hard I try."

After a month the Ugly Duckling waddled into the sunshine enjoying the breeze that ruffled his feathers.

He said to the hen and the cat, "Today I'm going to go swimming."

"Are you crazy?" said the hen. "You should be happy that you're in a warm, dry place. If you could do something useful, like lay eggs, you'd feel better about yourself. "

The cat added, "I hate the water! Why swim when you could stretch out in the sun and purr?"

"But it's so much fun to swim and dive to the bottom of the pond," said the Ugly Duckling.

The hen pecked at a bug and said, "Why aren't you happy with what you have here?"

"You don't understand," said the Ugly Duckling.

The old lady came around the back of the cottage carrying a basket. She praised the hen, saying, "My, what a fine egg you have laid this morning."

Then she bent down to pet the cat.

"My, what beautiful fur you have."

The cat smiled smugly at the Ugly Duckling and purred. Then he and the hen walked away without saying another word, leaving the Ugly Duckling alone.

The Ugly Duckling looked across the meadow. He could smell the water on the soft breeze. He felt tears in his eyes and a lump in his throat.

"Why can't I fit in?" he thought. "Why am I so different from everyone else?" He took one last look at the rickety old cottage, flapped his wings and rose into the air. In no time at all he found a pond where he could swim.

As the days went by the Ugly Duckling couldn't make friends with the other ducks who either made faces at him or ignored him. The air began to grow colder and the sky was full of clouds. A sharp wind rippled his feathers and sent yellow, orange, and scarlet leaves dancing off the trees. Soon there were as many leaves floating on the pond as there were sad thoughts about being different in the Ugly Duckling's head.

One evening when the sunset cast brilliant colors across the sky, he looked up and saw a flock of majestic white swans with long graceful necks fly overhead.

As he watched them disappear, the Ugly Duckling felt strange inside. He swam in circles, stretched his neck, and uttered a cry that was so strange it frightened him as it echoed across the water. He didn't know why, but he was drawn to those magnificent birds.

A few days later the pond grew bitter cold and the clouds finally let go of the snow they'd been saving. The Ugly Duckling swam in circles to stop the water around him from freezing, but during the night the ice kept creeping closer and closer. He tried to keep his legs moving, but he finally fell asleep, exhausted.

The next morning a farmer searching for firewood found the Ugly Duckling, his feet frozen in the pond. Carefully the farmer chipped away the ice with his axe and freed him. Then he put the Ugly Duckling in his coat and buttoned it tight.

Back home the farmer made a straw bed next to the fireplace and gently tucked the Ugly Duckling into it. Before long, the Ugly Duckling's feet began to feel better and he waddled up onto the fire place.

When the farmer's children saw the Ugly Duckling, they clapped their hands with joy. They wanted to play with him which made the Ugly Duckling happy because no one had ever wanted to play with him before.

Then he had a terrible thought. Perhaps they wanted to hurt him! He flapped his wings in terror, scattering straw across the room.

The farmer's wife screeched, "Catch that messy bird!"

The Ugly Duckling flew onto the kitchen table where the farmer's wife had been making bread. Flour began to rise up in huge clouds as the Ugly Duckling flapped his wings. The children were delighted, but their mother began waving her rolling pin at the frightened Ugly Duckling.

"Don't hurt him, Mama!" cried the oldest boy.

He quickly opened the front door and the Ugly Duckling flew out into the cold morning air.

For the rest of the winter the Ugly Duckling had to survive by eating what grain he could find. When spring returned, the Ugly Duckling stretched his wings which were stronger than before—and white—as white as the winter snow had been. One day, he heard trumpeting and looked up to see three swans gliding overhead.

Without thinking, he called out, and the swans circled around and landed on the water near the Ugly Duckling.

"What if they think I'm ugly and make fun of me?" he thought. "What if they bite me?"

Even though the Ugly Duckling was afraid, he held his head high and swam
toward the swans. They were beautiful, with sleek white feathers, slender long necks,
and black-and-orange bills. As he drew closer the Ugly Duckling lowered his head.

Then he saw a strange reflection in the water. Was there a fourth swan behind him?
He turned around, but saw no one. Then he looked again into the mirror-like water.

He realized that he was a swan—just like the three beautiful swans swimming toward him!
No wonder he'd never fit in with the ducks. He wasn't a duck—he was a swan.

Suddenly, the sound of laughter echoed across the pond.
The farmer's children had noticed the Ugly Duckling
and the other swans as they were fishing.

"Look, there's a new swan in the pond!"
shouted the oldest boy.

"He's even more beautiful than the
others," said a little girl with yellow braids.

Instantly the three other swans bowed
their heads in agreement.

The Ugly Duckling skittered across the water and flapped his wings with joy as he thought about all the things he'd gone through—being teased, bitten, and nearly frozen. Now someone was saying that he was the most beautiful of the swans. He fluffed his feathers, arched his graceful neck, and trumpeted for everyone to hear.

"I'm not an Ugly Duckling! I'm a beautiful swan."

Then he swam happily to the other swans knowing that he'd finally found where he truly belonged.

Character Building Questions and Activities

First I want to thank you for being concerned about the future of the children in your life. This section is a guide for helping your children become successful adults. Refer to it often, but don't try to complete the entire section in one or two sittings.

In the pages that follow are questions and activities you can do with your child. If you have a young child she/he might not be able to answer all the questions. That's okay. Later when they are older and have a problem with accepting the difference in themselves or dealing with someone who is bullying them, you can pull out this book and discuss the questions again.

The questions can also be changed to something that your child can relate to. Example from the harder questions in the Recognizing Differences section: How would the other kids treat you? To: How did Billy treat you the other day? Or How can you help another kid who was being treated badly? To: Kids don't seem to be nice to Sally. What is something nice you can do for her?

Remember: you're the greatest teacher your children will ever have and you can change their lives by simply helping them make healthy choices, feel better about themselves, and see the consequences of their actions and reactions to the people around them.

Enjoy this journey.

AnnaMarie

Character Building – Becoming Responsible

Discussion questions: Easy

What was Mother Duck feeling while she was sitting on her nest?
What would have happened to her eggs if she had left her nest to go play?
How was Mother Duck behaving by not leaving her nest?

Activities: Easy

1. What are your responsibilities? Is there a chore you have to do regularly?
Do you pick up your clothes? Do you put your toys away?
Show an adult what you do.
What good things happen when you complete that chore?
If you don't do that chore, what happens?

2. Put a sock on one hand and pretend it is the mother duck.
Use a basket or a bowl and pretend it is the nest. Put your sock hand on the nest.
Tell what the mother duck is thinking when she sits on the nest.
Move your hand away from the nest. Tell why the mother duck only moves away to eat
and is always in a hurry to return to the nest.

Discussion questions: Harder

If someone makes you so mad that you say something mean to them, who is in charge of how you respond?
Who has control over your life?

Activities: Harder

1. Blindfold your mother or father and then lead them around your house. How are you responsible for them?
How would you feel if someone was leading you around blindfolded and let you run into something?

2. What kind of a job would you like to have? Discuss or research with someone what kind of responsibilities that job has. Think about what you can do right now that would make you a better person for that job. Do you need to improve your math skills? Do you need to improve how you treat others? What books would a person with that type of job read?

"I take care of myself, because I learned early on that I'm the only person in life who's responsible for me"
Halle Berry

Character Building - Recognizing Differences

Discussion questions: Easy
Can you name three things that were the same for the Ugly
Duckling and his brothers and sisters when they were born?
How was the Ugly Duckling different from his brothers and sisters?
Think of someone very different from you.
How are the two of you different? How are you the same?

Activities: Easy
1. Find 5 pictures of people in magazincs who are different from you.
   Looking at the pictures, can you tell:
      Which person is the nicest? Why do you think so?
      Which person is the meanest? How do you know?
      Which one you'd like to have as a friend? Why?
      Do you think you can know what a person is really like by just looking at a picture?

2. Trace your child's hand on a piece of paper two times. For the first tracing have all of the fingers and the thumb spread out. This
will look more like a turkey. For the second tracing have the fingers together and the thumb spread out. This will look
more like a swan. Have your child color the spread out tracing as ugly as possible. Have your child color the second one
beautifully. Talk about how both are the same hand, but one looks ugly and one looks beautiful. Discuss that what is inside
is the most important, not how people see the outside.

Discussion questions: Harder
If you looked different from the other kids at school, how would you feel?
How would the other kids treat you?
How can you help another kid who was being treated badly?

Activities: Harder
1. Go to the library or on the Internet and look up a different country. Find pictures of the people. Make a list of how those people
are different and how they're the same as you. Which of your lists is longer?

2. Think about your best friend. Make a list of how you are alike. Make a list of how you are different. Tell why this is your best
friend

"The greatest gift that you can give to others is the gift of unconditional love and acceptance."
Brian Tracy.

Character Building – Preventing Bullying

Discussion questions: Easy
What would you do if you saw someone being picked on?
Has anyone ever picked on you?
What can you do to make them stop?

Activities: Easy
1. With an adult make a poster that describes a good friend.
Are you that type of friend? What can you do to be a better friend?

2. Pretend that you and your parent are actors in a play.
One person is a bully who takes your ball during recess and won't give
it back. Act out what you would say to the bully to change their behavior.
Then change roles.

Discussion questions: Harder
Did the Ugly Duckling deserve to be picked on?
What could the Ugly Duckling have done to stop it?
How can you protect yourself from a bully?

Activities: Harder
1. Make a list of the things bullies do to try to hurt other kids. Discuss why you think they pick on other people? What could be
happening at their home?

2. Watch the movie The Mighty distributed by Buena Vista Home Entertainment. How did Kevin and Max deal with the bullies?
How did their lives change when they became friends? What happened to make Max stand up to the bullies?

"Never be bullied into silence. Never allow yourself to be made a victim.
Accept no one's definition of your life, but define yourself."
Harvey S. Firestone

Character Building – Overcoming Loneliness

Discussion questions: Easy
When the Ugly Duckling was at the pond with the geese, why did he put mud on himself?
Why did the Ugly Duckling quickly wash off the mud after his encounter with the geese?
What are some things you can do when you're feeling lonely?

Activities: Easy
1. Make a mask out of paper or cardboard and then pretend to be something you're not while wearing your mask. What happens when you take the mask off? Was it fun to pretend to be something you're not? Do you like who you are without the mask?

2. A new student comes to your class and they don't know anyone. What are some things you can do to help that student, so they don't feel lonely?

Discussion questions: Harder
How does it feel when people don't pay attention to you?
Have you ever ignored someone, and how do you think it made them feel?
Do you ever think about changing yourself to fit in?

Activities: Harder
1. Make a friendship web. Put your name in the center of a piece of paper. Draw lines from your name and write the name of a friend on each line. Include your family.

2. Think of someone at school that everyone likes. Make a list of why the other kids like that person so much. Next, choose one of your friends and write a list of all the fun times you have had with that friend. Why do good memories help us not be lonely?

"I've learned that people will forget what you said, people will forget what you did,
but people will never forget how you made them feel."
Maya Angelou

Character Building – Being Happy to be You, Finding Self-Acceptance

Discussion questions: Easy
Why did the Ugly Duckling try to lay eggs and purr?
Did the fact that the Ugly Duckling couldn't purr or lay eggs mean he wasn't important?
Is there something that you really love to do? What is it?
How does that make you different from your friends?
Is it okay to be different?

Activities: Easy
1. Think of your favorite animal. Now pretend it was the only animal on Earth.
Make a list of what that would be like.
What would life be like if every human being was alike?

2. Tell about a time when you helped someone else and they thanked you.
How did you feel?

Discussion questions: Harder
If your friends can do things and you can't do them, does that mean you're not important?

Activities: Harder
1. Make a large flower out of construction paper. On each petal, write down one thing that makes you unique and special.
Ask your friends and family members what they think makes you special and unique, and add those things to the flower petals.
Put the flower on your bedroom door to remind you how special your really are.

2. Think of a favorite athlete in professional sports or in the Olympics. They don't win every game or medal yet they continue to compete. Write them a letter asking them what they do to overcome disappointments. Make a list of ways you can overcome disappointments. If you receive a letter back, see if there are any of his/her ways on your list.

"Someone's opinion of you does not have to become your reality."
Les Brown

Character Building – Being Brave/Being Fearful

Discussion questions: Easy
If you're scared to do something and you do it anyway, does that make you brave?
If you don't feel brave, does that mean you're not?
If you attempt to do something, even though you're scared, and fail, are you still brave?

Activities: Easy
1. Tell about your first day at school.
It was a very new place to be and you were brave.
How did you feel? What did you do?

2. Watch a movie with someone. Pause the movie when you see someone scared and discuss how she/he could be brave. When they have done something brave discuss if you could have done the same thing.

Discussion questions: Harder
What made the Ugly Duckling unhappy?
If the Ugly Duckling had stayed with the farmer's family, would he have been happy?
Would the winter have been easier if he'd stayed, and is doing the easy thing always the best choice?

Activities: Harder
1. Write a list of 5 things to be afraid of like spiders or bullies. Next to each one write the name of someone who isn't afraid or knows how to be brave. Find out which name to write by asking your family and your friends. As you write down their name, ask them why they are brave.

2. Choose one thing that you are afraid to do. Maybe it is taking a test. Maybe it is worrying about not being chosen to play on a team. Draw a cartoon. In the first frames show what it is you are afraid of. In the next frames show how you will handle the situation.

"Bravery is the capacity to perform properly even when scared half to death."
Omar Bradley

Character Building – Surviving Hardships

Discussion questions: Easy

Why did the ducklings need to break out of their shells?

What would have happened if one of the ducklings chose to stay inside its shell?

If your room was a shell, what would happen if you never left it?

Activities: Easy

1. Help your parent bake a cake that needs eggs.
Pretend that each egg contains a baby duck. Using a pen, tap the egg
gently until it breaks. Was it easy to crack the egg open?
Now tap part of the broken egg. Was it easier or harder to break?

2. Pretend that you have lost your favorite toy.
How does that make you feel? Draw a map of all the places you will look.
How does it make you feel to have a plan?

Discussion questions: Harder

What was the Ugly Duckling expecting when he saw the swans coming toward him?

What were the qualities that made the Ugly Duckling go on in spite of his problems?

Which of those qualities do you have?

Which of those qualities do you see in each of your family members?

Activities: Harder

1. Make a list of three things the Ugly Duckling experienced that caused him pain and sadness. How did those experiences feel to him? Ask two adults to tell you the most significant thing that threatened to stop them from achieving something they truly wanted to do. How did they overcome that thing?

2. In the news there are always people who have hardships. Read the newspaper or watch the news and find people who are having hardships. What can you do to help them?

"Happiness can be found, even in the darkest of times, if one only remembers to turn on the light."
Steven Kloves (Dumbledore), Harry Potter and the Prisoner of Azkaban (Movie)

Responsibility

What was Mother Duck feeling while she was sitting on the nest?
Frustrated and tired. She wanted her eggs to hatch to see her children.

What could have happened to her eggs if she had left her nest to go play?
An animal could have eaten them or stole them.
They could have gotten cold and never hatched.

How was the mother duck behaving by not leaving her nest?
Responsible

Who is responsible for what you do?
You are.

If someone makes you so mad that you say something mean to them, who is in charge of how you respond?
You are the only one who can open your mouth and make you talk.
If you choose to say something mean, you're the only one responsible.

Who has control over your life?
Only you, especially when you get older. You're the only one who chooses what to do with your life.

Differences

Can you name three things that were the same for the Ugly Duckling and his brothers and sisters when they were born?
They all had to crack their shells before they could start coming out.
They all made pecking sounds while they were trying to get out.
They all worked hard to break out of their shells.
Mother Duck quacked encouragingly for all of them.

How was the Ugly Duckling different from his brothers and sisters?
He was a different color and much larger.

Think of someone different from you. How are the two of you different and how are you the same?
This answer will vary with every child and the friend being chosen.

If you looked different from the other kids at school, how would you feel?
This answer will vary with each child.

How would the other kids treat you?
Some would treat you well, but others might pick on you.

How can you help another kid who was being treated badly?
Talk to them and make them feel accepted.

Bullying

What would you do if you saw someone being picked on?
Help them if you can.

Has anyone ever picked on you?
The answer will vary from child to child.

What can you do to make them stop?
Speak up for yourself.
Act like you are not afraid.

Did the Ugly Duckling deserve to be picked on?
No one ever deserves to be picked on.

What could the Ugly Duckling have done to stop it?
Nothing, because it was the results of someone else's poor choices.

How can you protect yourself from a bully?
1. Discuss ways to avoid coming in contact with that person.
2. Stand tall and act brave even if you don't feel like it. How would your favorite actor/actress behave if they were being bullied? Pretend to be that person.
3. Spend time doing something you love to do. It will build up your confidence as you get better at it.
4. Take a class that teaches you how to defend yourselves.
5. Practice things you can say to a bully.

Loneliness

When the Ugly Duckling was at the pond with the geese, why did he put mud on himself?
He was hoping to change his appearance so he'd fit in and be accepted.

Why did the Ugly Duckling quickly wash off the mud after his encounter with the geese?
He didn't want to be shot at. Trying to act and look like something you aren't can be very dangerous.

What are some things you can do when you're feeling lonely?
The answer will vary according to each child's interest, ability, and temperament.

How does it feel when people don't pay attention to you?
It probably hurt and made you feel sad, and it might even have made you angry.

Have you ever ignored someone, and how do you think it made them feel?
They probably felt exactly the same way you would.

Do you ever think about changing yourself to fit in?
The answers will vary according to each child.

Self-Acceptance

Why did the Ugly Duckling try to lay eggs and purr?
He wanted to be like the cat and hen.

Did the fact that the Ugly Duckling couldn't purr or lay eggs mean he wasn't important?
No, he could swim and do other things that the hen and cat couldn't do.

Is there something that you really love to do?
Every child's interests will be unique to them.

How does that make you different from your friends?
This will vary according to each child.

Is it okay to be different than others?
Absolutely! In fact, there's no way we could all be the same!

If your friends can do things you can't, does that mean you're not important?

No, because you're different than anyone else. You're unique and special.

Bravery and Fearfulness

If you're scared to do something and you do it anyway, does that make you brave?
Absolutely!

If you don't feel brave, does that mean you're not?
No, you're still brave. Sometimes our feelings lie.

If you attempt to do something, even though you're scared, and fail, are you still brave?
Yes, because it's not failure or success that makes you brave.
It's making the attempt, even when you're scared, that makes you brave.

What made the Ugly Duckling unhappy?
The painful memories of his past and the fear of being hurt again.
Fear of the future.

If the Ugly Duckling had stayed with the farmer's family, would he have been happy?
Yes, because he would have had shelter, warmth, food, and children who loved him.

Would the winter have been easier if he'd stayed, and is doing the easy thing always the best choice?
That winter would have been easier, but doing the easiest thing isn't always the best choice.
You often have to work hard for the things you really want.

Hardship

Why did the ducklings need to break out of their shells?
They couldn't continue to grow if they had stayed inside.
They would eventually die if they didn't break out.

What would have happened if one of the ducklings had chosen to stay inside its shell?
It would have died.
It would never be able to experience the beauty of life.
It would never be able to make friends with the swans.

If your room was a shell, what would happen if you never left it?
You and the room would get stinky. Where would you go to the bathroom or take a shower?
You wouldn't have any friends.
You'd never experience the outside world.

What was the Ugly Duckling expecting when he saw the swans coming toward him?
He was expecting to be bitten, since so many bad things had happened to him in the past.

What were the qualities that made the Ugly Duckling go on in spite of his problems?
He never let life "just happen." He took control and tried to make the most of each situation he faced.

Which of those qualities do you have?
The answer will vary according to your child's ability, interests, and temperament.

Which of those qualities do you see in each of your family members?
This answer will be as unique as the family.

Continuing Character Building.

Use the concepts from this story every day. Give your child verbal encouragement based on the character building traits they have discussed.

Here are some sample comments:

Thank you for being so responsible, just like Mother Duck was with her eggs.
I know you were tired, but you did your chores anyway. I'm very proud of you.
You're such a responsible person. Thank you.
Way to go for trying something new!
That experience was just like a shell, but you broke through it. Nice job!
You didn't play the victim. That's awesome!
It was brave of you to stand up for that person.
I saw you being nice to that person. Great job!
You've given that person a great gift by offering your love and friendship.
I'm so glad you don't try to be like everyone else.
I could see you wanted to say something mean, but you didn't. You're remarkable!
I know you feel lonely right now, like the Ugly Duckling, but you'll find your way, just like he did.
It's okay if you can't do what your friend can do. You're unique and different. Why don't you practice_____?
You have a gift for that.
You're so valuable to me.
"That kid was picking on you because you're different, just like the Ugly Duckling was, but he survived and turned into a beautiful swan—and you're an awesome person, too."
Just like the Ugly Duckling couldn't lay eggs, you can't do _____, but let's talk about what you are good at and work on that.
I'm so proud of you for attempting to do what you were afraid to do. That was very brave.
You were afraid, but you did it anyway.
You're becoming a beautiful swan

For Information on our Free Downloads
and other products visit our website at
www.successfulkidspublishing.com

A Portion of Each Book Sold is Donated to
Dream for Kids

Dreams for Kids, an international youth empowerment and children rights organization, is a registered nonprofit, 501(c) (3), children's charity whose mission is to empower young people of all abilities through dynamic leadership programs and life-changing activities that inspire them to fearlessly pursue their dreams and compassionately change the world.

Dreams for Kids was born on December 24, 1989, in a small room inside a homeless shelter in Chicago, in a place called Clara's House. A holiday party for 54 homeless children and their families has grown into an international day of giving and hope for communities around the world. Today, Holiday for Hope is the largest annual holiday event of its kind in the world, serving over 1,200 children in need in the Chicago area alone, as well as thousands more internationally.

By the year 2006, Dreams for Kids programs had impacted the lives of over 25,000 children. However, it was when the story of the organization was written that a global movement began. Kiss of a Dolphin, the story of Dreams for Kids, written by Tom Tuohy, and published in November 2006, tells this magical story and also the stories of inspiration and generosity which have made Dreams for Kids the organization it is today.

Dreams for Kids programs have expanded and grown over the years. Extreme Recess!, began in 1996, and brings children with physical and developmental challenges from the sidelines of life and gives them opportunities to participate in the activities of their dreams, such as kayaking, water and snow skiing, sled hockey, horseback riding, basketball, rock climbing, sailing, and more.

Dream Leaders, is a youth leadership program which works with schools and youth organizations, in partnership with government and social agencies, bringing diverse groups of young people together to work on cooperative projects which serve the local and world communities, and giving them the opportunity to become citizens of the world.

The Dreams for Kids Global Village is a powerful and innovative way for youth and community organizations to "Adopt a Dream" and eliminate the isolation of children with disabilities in their local neighborhood, and provide freedom and education for child laborers in developing countries.

 Dreams for Kids Dolphin Spirit Programs reach across the globe to impact children of all abilities, and of every gender, race, religious and socio-economic background. Dreams for Kids programs eliminate the isolation of children, empower them to live the life they have imagined, and inspire them to live a life of service. www.dreamsforkids.org 1-866-729-5454.